KEEPING SECRETS

Jenny Koralek ~ Steve Cox

BLue Bananas

KEEPING SECRETS

Jenny Koralek ~ Steve Cox

MAMMOTH

Titles in the series:

Big Dog and Little Dog Visit the Moon
The Nut Map
Dilly and the Goody-Goody
Tom's Hats
Juggling with Jeremy
Baby Bear Comes Home
The Magnificent Mummies
Mouse Flute
Delilah Digs for Treasure
Owl in the House
Runaway Fred
Keeping Secrets

First published in Great Britain 1997
by Heinemann and Mammoth, imprints of Reed International Books Ltd
Michelin House, 81 Fulham Road, London SW3 6RB
and Auckland, Melbourne, Singapore and Toronto
Text copyright © Jenny Koralek 1997
Illustrations copyright © Steve Cox 1997
The Author and Illustrator have asserted their moral rights
Paperback ISBN 0 7497 2812 4
Hardback ISBN 0 434 97478 1
1 3 5 7 9 10 8 6 4 2
A CIP catalogue record for this title
is available from the British Library
Produced by Mandarin Offset Ltd
Printed and bound in China

Rosie Mundy lived with her mum and dad and her rag doll, Mona Liz. One morning Rosie Mundy's dad ran into the kitchen waving an envelope. 'We've won! We've won!' he shouted to Mum.

'What have you won?' asked Rosie.

'A competition!' said Dad.

'For a holiday in Paris for two!'

said Mum.

'But,' wailed Rosie Mundy, 'who will

look after me?'

'You can go and stay with Aunt Jobiska

and the boys!' said Dad.

'Can I?' said Rosie happily.

Are you sure?

'Of course she can!' said Aunt Jobiska, when Mum rang to ask her.

'So get packing!'

Rosie packed her own bag and

a small one for Mona Liz too.

Straight after breakfast on Saturday they
drove off to Aunt Jobiska's. She was
standing at the gate to meet them.

Rosie loved Aunt Jobiska, who kept
ducks and wove rugs and wore long
skirts and was hardly ever cross.

The boys have been cooking.

Josh and Harry were excited to see Rosie. They had made a big chocolate cake. Everyone had two slices of cake before Rosie's mum and dad said goodbye.

Later, when Aunt Jobiska went to

feed her three ducks, the boys looked

at Rosie solemnly.

'Can you keep a secret?' they asked.

'I don't know. . .' stammered Rosie.

'Well,' said Josh, 'we'd better find out!

Come and see us tonight after lights out,

and don't eat too much supper!'

At supper Aunt Jobiska was worried when Rosie said she did not want any pudding.

The boys' secret was a midnight feast
of doughnuts full of jam and fizzy apple
juice and playing 'Snap' in whispers.

17

All next day the boys watched and waited for Rosie to give away their secret, but her mouth stayed closed and her eyes said nothing.

'Better see if she can keep one more secret,' said Josh to Harry, 'before we let her in on the **BIG** one!'

The next day they took Rosie up to the attic.

They knelt down on the floor, lifted up a
floorboard and pulled out some things
wrapped up in bits of old torn sheets.
'Look!' whispered Harry. 'I've made this
for Mum's birthday!'

20

Harry uncovered a painting he had done of the sea. The sun was shining down on a little boat with two boys in it. The boat was riding green waves with frilly white edges.

'Mum loves the sea,' said Harry, 'so this picture will make her happy. Go on, Josh! Unwrap *your* present.'

Josh carefully unfolded a small round box and held it up. It was covered with sea shells – little, pearly, round ones and sharper, larger, yellow ones.

In the middle of the lid was the biggest

shell of all. 'Yes, Mum loves the sea,'

sighed Josh, 'and so do we...'

At suppertime Aunt Jobiska said,

'You look a bit dusty, Rosie.

Did you have fun in the attic?'

'Yes,' said Rosie.

'Hmmm. . .' said Aunt Jobiska. 'You look more like Mona Liz every day. Your big eyes tell no tales and your mouth looks as if it has been sewn up with thread!'

And she went away to weave a rug.

Well done, Rosie!

You've passed the test.

Next morning Josh said, 'Come with us,

Rosie, but don't bring that doll!'

'Why not?' wailed Rosie Mundy.

'Because you will need free hands

if you want to get to our biggest

secret safely,' added Harry.

Rosie followed the boys down through

the long garden until they came to a

small hole in the hedge.

Rosie Mundy crawled after the boys, through the small hole into the rambly, brambly garden of the house next door.

'The house is empty,' said Josh,

'because it's up for sale.'

'Now we're going to let you in

on our BIG secret,' said Harry.

Josh and Harry led Rosie to a huge

oak tree with strong, friendly branches.

A sturdy wooden ladder rested against

the thick trunk. Above them the green

leaves rustled in the wind.

'I'll go first,' said Harry, 'then you in the middle, Rosie, like jam in a sandwich. Josh will come last.' Slowly, carefully, Rosie and the boys began to climb.

Up and up they climbed, through the
whispering tree, until they came to a
huge fork in the branches.

33

Rosie saw a wide platform.
In the middle of it there
was a house with a roof,
windows and a door.
'Ohh!' she breathed.
Rosie gazed up through
the rustling leaves.
'A secret house!' she said.
'No, a secret boat,'
said Harry.

'Come into the cabin!'

Rosie followed the boys into the boat.

'It's got curtains and cushions!' said

Rosie. 'And dominoes!'

'And crayons and paper!' said Josh.

'And books for rainy days!'

36

'But that's not all!' said Harry. 'Josh, show

Rosie the telescope and the shell...'

The tclescope was a long, cardboard roll, painted black and gold.

The shell was large and pink, like the roses in Aunt Jobiska's garden...

'With this telescope,' said Harry,

'you can see for miles across the ocean.

Come onto the deck and try it!'

But when Rosie held the telescope

to one eye all she could see was a

sea of green, waving tree-tops.

And when she held the shell hard against her ear all she could hear was the sighing, singing, of the sea.

After a long time aloft, Rosie and the boys climbed carefully down the ladder again. 'Remember,' said Josh, 'you mustn't tell anyone about our big secret.'

'I promise!' said Rosie.

I'll never tell anyone.

At suppertime, Aunt Jobiska said,

'You look a bit muddy, Rosie.

Did you have fun in the garden?'

'Yes,' said Rosie.

'Hmm,' said Aunt Jobiska.

43

The next morning, Josh and Harry woke

Rosie. They shouted excitedly, 'Come

and look, quickly!'

In the garden of the house next door
stood a huge boat. They could see
Aunt Jobiska stroking a big yellow
dog and talking to a man.

'Come and meet our new neighbour,
Mr Dillon and his dog, Goldie!'
she called.

Mr Dillon smiled at the children as they dashed through the gate. 'You can come and play with Goldie anytime,' he said.

'Great!' said Harry.

'And *now*,' said Mr Dillon, 'who'd like to come sailing with me tomorrow?'

'Me! Me! Me!' they all shouted.

In bed that night Rosie hugged Mona Liz and whispered, 'I don't care what the boys say, you are definitely coming with us tomorrow.'

And she went to sleep dreaming of ships in trees and ships on water.